The Cat That Purred

Written by
John J. Piantedosi

Illustrated by
Andrea Maglio-Macullar

NCP
New City Press
of the Focolare
Hyde Park, New York

Published in the United States by New City Press
202 Comforter Blvd., Hyde Park, NY 12538
www.newcitypress.com

Illustrations by Andrea Maglio-Macullar

Cover design by Leandro DeLeon
Layout design by Steven Cordiviola

ISBN: 978-1-56548-540-2

Printed in the United States

Lovingly Dedicated to my Godson Nikolai:

May you always know when to lead and when to follow in a life full of enthusiasm, compassion, and joy.

Your Godfather, John

Once upon a time, there was a cat,

who loved to purr and that was that.

He purred and purred and purred all day.

He never meowed; he never played.

One summer as he purred away,

a dog drew near and asked to play.

"Good cat, let us go skip and run.

I'm sure that we'll have lots of fun!"

"No thank you, sir," the cat replied.

"I cannot skip or run outside.

I purr and purr and purr all day.

I do not have the time to play."

The dog let out a gentle bark;

then sadly wandered to the park.

The cat laid down and purred some more.

He purred and purred a gentle roar.

So sad he sat alone all day,

afraid to skip and run and play.

"I am so small; I can't compete

with dogs that have much bigger feet!"

"In summer sun I'd love to play!

Perhaps I will another day!"

One autumn as he purred away,

a squirrel drew near and asked to play.

"Good cat, come let's go climb and hide.

It's autumn now; it's cool outside.

If we together take a run,

then we'll stay warm and have some fun.

I'll show you where I hide my food,

for wintertime can be so rude,

with winds so strong they roar and blow,

with icicles and fluffy snow."

"No thank you, ma'am," the cat replied.

"I don't know how to climb and hide.

I purr and purr and purr all day.

I do not have the time to play."

The squirrel let out a gentle squeal,

then wandered off with wagging tail.

The cat laid down and purred some more.

He purred and purred a gentle roar.

So sad he sat alone all day,

afraid to climb and hide and play.

"My claws are short for climbing trees!

My fur is thin; I fear I'd freeze!

I'd rather purr and purr all day.

I haven't got the time to play!

In autumn sun I'd love to play!

Perhaps I will another day!"

In winter as he purred away,

a bear drew near and asked to play.

"Good cat, let us go hunt and roar.

I cannot sleep; my neighbors snore!

Let's find a snack to hold us through

the chill of winter; nuts won't do!

Let's roar and roar and roar and roar!

We'll tease our neighbors evermore!"

"No thank you, sir," the cat replied.

"I do not hunt or roar outside.

I purr and purr and purr all day.

I do not have the time to play."

The bear let out a gentle roar.

It sounded like a muffled snore.

He slowly waddled through the snow,

as if he had no place to go.

The cat laid down and purred some more.

He purred and purred a gentle roar.

So sad he sat alone all day,

afraid to hunt and roar and play.

"I cannot hunt! I cannot roar!

I purr and purr and purr some more.

I wish I could! I wish I might!

I'm scared! I'm scared! I'm full of fright!"

"In winter sun I'd love to play!

Perhaps I will another day!"

One spring as he purred away,

a bird drew near and asked to play.

"Good cat, let us go fly and sing!

Winter's gone! It's finally spring!"

"No thank you, ma'am," the cat replied.

"I cannot fly or sing outside.

I purr and purr and purr all day.

I do not have the time to play."

The bird let out a high pitched squeal.

"Come now, good cat, let's get real!

I know you purr and purr all day.

I know you haven't time to play.

You fear to skip and run outside.

You even fear to climb and hide.

I know you fear to hunt and roar

and now you fear to sing and soar!

You sing all day with gentle purr,

alone and sad you may prefer.

Good cat, please join our band of four.

We need your purr to make us soar!"

"You see our dog can only bark.

He plays piano in the park.

You see our squirrel can only squeal.

She plays guitar with strings of steel.

You see our bear can only roar.

He plays the drums. His timing's poor.

You see I sing and sing and sing.

I don't read music; that's the thing!

We need you, cat, to lead our band.

That purr of yours is simply grand!

That purr of yours will keep the beat.

A little meow would be a treat!"

"I thank you ma'am," the cat replied.

"Now I can fly and sing outside!

I purred and purred and purred all day;

but now I have the time to play!"

The cat stood up and purred some more.

He purred and purred a happy roar.

So happy he had time to play;

no longer all alone all day.

"So what I'm small," the cat meowed.

"I'll lead the band! We'll please the crowds!

Through summer, autumn, winter, spring,

our music fit for queens and kings!

In springtime sun we'll play and play!

No more 'perhaps another day!'"

ABOUT THE AUTHOR: John J. Piantedosi has been a religious educator for about twenty-five years as a high school teacher, a campus minister, and a catechetical leader. He holds a Master's of Education in Counseling from Boston State College and a Master's of Arts in Ministry from St John's Seminary. Presently, John is an Adjunct Professor of Behavioral Studies, History/Government and Learning Communities at Bunker Hill Community College in the Boston area. He is also the author of *The Gospel for Children*, published by New City Press, 2011.

ABOUT THE ILLUSTRATOR: Andrea Maglio-Macullar is an artist, painter, designer, illustrator and writer. Her education includes studying at Northeastern University and then continuing on to Monserrat College of Art and The De Cordova Museum School. She has won many awards for her paintings and has illustrated and/or written several books about the Saints and Popes and children's stories. She is the author of *The Rosary for Children* published by Our Sunday Visitor. You can see more of her work at www.andsart.weebly.com. She lives in Massachusetts with her husband Bill.

NEW CITY PRESS
of the Focolare
Hyde Park, New York

New City Press is one of more than 20 publishing ses sponsored by the Focolare, a movement founded Chiara Lubich to help bring about the realization esus' prayer: "That all may be one" (John 17:21). In v of that goal, New City Press publishes books and urces that enrich the lives of people and help all to ve toward the unity of the entire human family. We a member of the Association of Catholic Publishers.

Further Reading
All titles are available from New City Press.

www.NewCityPress.com

ne the Elephant	978-1-56548-450-4	$9.95
dy's Little Kite	978-1-56548-528-0	$11.95
e Gospel for Children	978-1-56548-370-5	$13.95

Scan to join our mailing list for discounts and promotions or go to

www.newcitypress.com

and click on "join our email list."

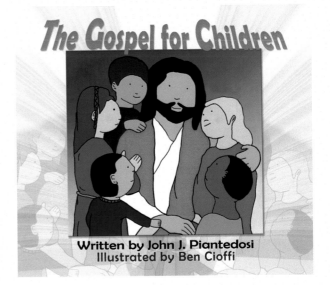

The Gospel for Children
Written by John J. Piantedosi
Illustrated by Ben Cioffi

Written in a charming rhyming style and featuring brightly-colored illustrations, *The Gospel for Children* introduces preschool and middle-school-aged children to Jesus through the major events in his life.

Other Material of Interest
available at www.livingcitymagazine.com
The Cube of Love and *The Cube of Peace*
(starting at $7.95)

The Cubes are a simple, innovative way to transform individual behavior and group dynamics into harmonious reciprocal relations that foster universal brotherhood. Children learn how to resolve conflicts and create a new culture based on mutual respect and concern becoming co-builders of peace.

Living City Magazine

A magazine that shows that unity is possible among diverse people in many circumstances of everyday life.